**HANS SANDE** (born 1946) is a prize-winning Norwegian writer, painter and psychiatrist, with more than 50 published books, including novels and short stories, poetry and drama, as well as books for children.

**MARIETTA TARALRUD MADDRELL** was born in England to Scandinavian parents and only began translating from Norwegian and Swedish after chance meetings in India with Hindi poets. Her translations include *Voices from Chernobyl* (2009) and *Here Lay Tirpitz* (2022), both by Ingrid Storholmen, and *Lynette's Journey* (2014) by Hanne Bramness.

## Praise for *Black Calf @ White Snow*

'While the love between mother and son is extremely human, their conditions of life underscore...the merciless dictates of efficient production. [This book] is amusing, risky and absurd, but also painful and serious. Recommended to everyone who likes something heartwarming, bizarre and astonishing.'—*Aftenposten*

'*Black Calf @ White Snow* explores important aspects of life, for both cattle and humans, and addresses itself to readers of all ages.'—*Bergens Tidende*

# Black Calf @ White Snow

an email novel

## Hans Sande

Translated from the NORWEGIAN by
**Marietta Taralrud Maddrell**
Illustrated by **Per Dybvig**

Series editor **Teji Grover**

YATRA BOOKS
An imprint of Vani Prakashan Group

WHITE NIGHTS SERIES

vaniprakashan.com

First Edition : 2023

Yatra Books is an imprint of Vani Prakashan Group

Head Office

4695, 21-A, Daryaganj, New Delhi-110 002, India
Phone : +91 11 23273167, 23275710

Registered Bookstores and Offices

*Ashok Rajpath, Patna-800 004, Bihar*
*Coffee House Campus, Mahatma Gandhi Marg, Allahabad-211 001, Uttar Pradesh*
*Mahatma Gandhi International Hindi University, Wardha-442 001, Maharashtra*
*36-A, Shakespeare Sarani, Near Rani Birla Girls College, Kolkata-700017, West Bengal*

sales@vaniprakashan.in
vaniprakashan@gmail.com

Black Calf @ White Snow

NORLA Norwegian Literature Abroad

This translation has been published with the financial support of NORLA (Norwegian Literature Abroad) foundation.

First published in Norwegian as *Svart kalv @ kvit snø* by N.W. Damm & Søn


ISBN : 978-93-5518-911-0
Fiction



*Printed and bound in India at Thomson Press (India) Ltd.*

*We must never be afraid to go too far,*
*because truth always lies beyond.*

The Great Bull Proust

DEAR MOTHER

I have decided to run away. Sinister things are happening here on the farm, but nobody talks about them. I dare not stay here any longer. Dare not wait and see what is going to happen to me. I don't want to be disappeared suddenly.
Love from me

MY DEAR LITTLE BOY

But now you *have* disappeared suddenly! How could you think of going away from your mother? And without saying a word! You can't just run off like that without saying goodbye! Have you forgotten all I have done for you? Have you forgotten that it was I who gave birth to you? Have you forgotten how cosy we were together, and the warm milk you drank from my teats?
Love from Mother

DEAR MOTHER

No, I haven't forgotten. Look, you see I call you 'dear Mother'? I haven't forgotten your good smell and the soft teats and the sweet taste of your milk. But it is a long time since I was allowed to drink it. You know that very well, so why are you making things up? You know that only a couple of days after I was born, the farmer came with a pail instead. And was I allowed to stay with you? Oh no! I had to stand in a calf pen with the other calves. However much I whimpered and bellowed, I wasn't allowed to get close to you anymore. I haven't forgotten that.

I got yellow tags in my ears. Stinging and bleeding. I was given a pail. And the mixture I was given to drink was either too cold or too warm. What was this? I wanted to go on sucking! But the only things I got to suck on were the fingers of the farmer's wife, the farmer and their children. I sucked and sucked at all the fingers I came across but nothing came out. Still I couldn't stop sucking. I haven't forgotten that either.
Love from Krollalfa*

DEAR SON

Such is life. What we long for, we only get to taste for a brief second. Then it is over. The rest of the time we can only dream about the good things. Think of the good moments we had together! Think of the time before they came and took you away from me! You must not suppose it was easy for me either. Do you think I don't remember your complaining? I was so upset that I myself nearly forgot to eat. But you drank your fill every day. Yes, you ate and drank and stuffed yourself, I saw it. The farmer came and gave you everything you need to grow strong. But what do you have to eat now? Who is taking care of you?

Come home! You mustn't go away from me, you too! Think of all the calves I have had over the years!
Love from Mamma

---

* In Norwegian, the @ sign is called 'Krollalfa', literally 'Curly Alpha'.

DEAR MOTHER

Yes, where are they? Answer me that, then I may come home again, maybe.

Love from your boy

MY DEAR LITTLE BULL

But how are you going to manage out there in the wilderness? What are you going to live on, and who are you going to have for company? You must have understood this, that we can't manage without people. Our farmer is really fond of us and takes good care of us in every way. You are so young and thoughtless! If you had only stayed here with the rest of us for another couple of months, then you would have realized it, you too.

Love from a very anxious Mother

DEAR MOTHER

I don't think you are telling the truth now. The farmer seems to be kind, but I don't trust him. You surely know there are ugly rumours about what happens to us. Particularly to us bull calves. Say it now, and be honest! What has happened to all the other stalwart sons you told me about?

Love from me

MY DEAR BOY

I well understand that you are confused. But you must not think badly of those who are closest to you. My sons are out in the world, grazing in green meadows. There really are places on earth where the grass is green all the year round, and where animals can walk about outside and graze and be free. One of those places is called Africa. My sons mix with wild cattle which roam around in large herds, highborn cattle which are silver-grey in appearance, and they produce splendid calves the likes of which nobody has seen here in the north.

There is no snow or winter there. The grass is so high that you can hide yourself in it, and so juicy that you hardly need to drink. But if you get thirsty anyway, there are plenty of streams and rivers winding through all the greenery, with clear fresh water. There are no people in Africa, and no fences, no stalls. All kinds of animals walk about freely, and the air is full of birds of all colours. In Africa all have plenty of both food and drink all the year round. So don't come here with nasty thoughts about my other sons.
Love from Mother

DEAR MOTHER

I don't know whether it is true, what you say. Why is it only bulls who can travel there? Something is not quite right, and surely you must notice it as well. But I can easily travel to Africa and find out. It's beginning to get cold at night up here on the mountain. Every night I creep in and hide myself among some thick bushes. But it is so cold that I have to jump out at once and run around to warm up. But in the

daytime it's fine. I have searched for the high pasture you told me about. But I haven't found it yet.
Love from your son (the living one)

DEAR SON

To reach the high pasture you have to go upwards along the river and get your bearings from the mountain on which the sun rests in the middle of the day. After a while you come to a bridge made of planks. It feels scary to walk across, but I don't think it's dangerous. At any rate we have gone over it in droves, and the farmer followed across with horse and cart. That time when he had a horse and cart. But my dear, what are you doing up there now that winter is approaching? You don't even know what winter is, you innocent little calf!
Your Mother

WELL MOTHER

Now I don't understand anything! Can't I rely on what you tell me? You said, didn't you, that at the high pasture the grass is always fresh and green, and the air is so nice and warm that they can lie outside at night! And you said they waded across the river without feeling cold. And that they lay in the sun relaxing and chewing the cud for hours on end.
Love from your bewildered son

DEAR KROLLALFA

I can well believe you are bewildered. You are so young, after all, and know nothing about the seasons. You were born in spring like all my other calves, and you have only experienced the cowshed and a summer in the fields just outside the barn. But now it is several years since we grownups were at the high pasture in the summers. And summer, that's the warm season. Right after summer comes autumn. It is the same every year. And with autumn at our heels we simply had to plod down again from the high pasture and get under a roof here in the cowshed. Yes, the warm summer was quickly devoured. Then the green grass and wandering in freedom was over. Yeah, we walked around freely until the dairymaid perched up on a hillock and called out.

'Come on, cows! Come on, cows!' she called. 'Come now, my Plomma and Dokka, come now, Fagerlin and Venelin and Gullsid, come now, Bota and Veslemoy, and you too, Krollbrura,* my dearest cow, coooome along, then!'

The dairymaid called as she had done all summer. But now it was for the last time, we could hear it in her voice and we felt it inside ourselves as we came ambling along in a line. Yes, we knew that winter was soon coming to chase us down to the village by force, if we did not go willingly.

That's how it was then, and that's how it is now. Now winter is approaching again, and I hardly dare imagine how you will get by! Winter is icy cold, the grass soon withers and gets covered with snow and ice. No, you don't know what that is. But the world you know will be hidden under a layer of cold. Then you have to be here in the

* 'Curly Bride'.

warmth of the cowshed to survive. Try to understand that you are not made for walking about outside in nature in winter! Winter kills slowly, but surely, everything that can't hide itself in thick fur or warm feathers. How are you going to hide yourself? Do you have fur or feathers? No, you have to hide yourself here at home with your mother!
Love from your Mother, in despair

DEAR MOTHER

I'm staying here anyway! I followed the route you explained to me, along the river and over the bridge, and at last I found my way to the high pasture. Yes, it is fine up here, as free as you said. I can go in and out of the little cowshed, and the grass is still green. But tell me, doesn't this grass taste different from the grass at home? Stronger, wilder?

And guess who I met yesterday? Wild sheep! Yes. I've become acquainted with some wild sheep, and they have

said I can stay with them through the winter. I am sure to be alright.
A hug from your son

DEAR SON

No, now you have to listen to your mother! A sheep is a sheep, and a calf is a calf! Can't you see that the sheep have wool? Particularly wild sheep, which have never lived in a house and close to people. They live outside!

They have found a way of surviving out there, and they huddle close together, so that they can warm each other. But you are only a poor crazy bull calf who knows next to nothing about life! I am so afraid that you will be cold and hungry and, in the end, kick the bucket! Down here you will have everything you need. Food and warmth and safety, day and night. Come home, now!
Mother

HI MOTHER

Try to get into your skull that I have made up my mind, and it is for real. I would rather live and die up here on the mountain as a free bull, than be fetched and slaughtered and eaten up by the farmer and other people. Do you know what the word 'chop' means? And 'beef'?
Love from your son, who is alive

MY DEAR LITTLE BULL CALF

Don't use such nasty words! I can well understand that you are confused and scared. But in any case, everyone lives only as long as the farmer wishes. This is called animal life on the farm. And you have to learn that you are only one among thousands of domestic animals who are well cared for and get everything they need, right up to the end. You can't do anything about it. It is not in our power to change it. You simply have to enjoy the warmth and the food and the kind words you may get from the farmer as long as they last. Anyway, it doesn't help if you begin speaking bad words and being cheeky to your mother.

Love from your ever-loving Mother

DEAR MOTHER

Alright, I won't be cheeky to you and I won't use bad words. We must enjoy the warmth and food and kind words as long as they last, you say. Yes, but for how long? And why don't you dare tell me what happens afterwards? Why don't you like me asking? How else am I going to find out? I would have liked to ask you what the expression 'fatted calf' means, but I'll let it be. You can get shivers down your spine from those words. I will only say that it would be good for me if you were honest and told me what is really ahead of us. Right up till now I thought you were blind. Or simply as stupid as a fly. And isn't it probably better to be able to talk about it than just go on brooding on our own?

This is what I am wondering about: Is it that we children ask and ask right up until we have nothing more to ask about? Have we then become grownup cows and bulls who just lie regurgitating the same thoughts? Do the grownups keep chewing thoughts up into little pieces and swallowing them down and shitting the remains out again as cowpats? And carry on while they wonder what it was they used to wonder about once?

DEAR OBSTINATE SON

Now you are talking above yourself and well above my head. Imagining that we chew and regurgitate and chew and swallow our own thoughts gets us nowhere. You must leave aside such preaching and learn to enjoy life. We don't need all that much. A good bundle of hay, fresh water and a few kind words from the farmer. That's enough for a day. Perhaps to top it all he scratches our heads a little. The rest of the time we can dream good dreams.
Your Mother

DEAR MOTHER

Thanks for your reply. It was as I thought. But I can't be bothered to listen to that sort of thing! I will not live in that way. Listen to this, then! I have become good friends with the sheep now. The language of sheep is not at all difficult. Sheep bleat and we moo, that is so. But we speak in the same way with our bodies, even though they can't use their tails like us. They can't whip their tails about or scratch themselves on the belly. But I'm sure you don't expect me to look down on them for these reasons? Sheep shit small hard balls instead of wet cakes. Why is that? I wonder about it. We eat the same grass, after all. I asked one of the ewes about it, and she said it was a mystery!

Confused son

GIVE UP, BOY!

So this is a kind of mystery? I told the other cows, and they laughed themselves silly. What sort of son have you raised, they sneered. Is he the revolutionary who roamed out into the world to solve the great mystery of sheep droppings and cowpats?

What a numbskull! Give up, boy! Now I am completely

ruined because of you. I who was once the bell cow!
Disappointed Mother

OH MOTHER!

Don't bother about what others say! Just let them stand there in their collars and chains and laugh at me! Let them be numbskulls themselves! I live and wonder about so many things! Nothing is too small or too big for me! And it really is a mystery, about the sheep droppings!
Free son

LITTLE IDIOT

No, it isn't a mystery. Everyone with any experience of life knows that if sheep get plenty of grass, they shit cakes too, small cakes, true enough, but cakes all the same. And if they have to nibble and struggle to get enough, they will shit balls.

That's how it is. Now you can come home again. The mystery is solved. (You could simply have asked me.)
Mother

OH?

Could I? You must be grumpy because I am wondering about everything between heaven and earth and can't keep my thoughts to myself! My best friends are two lambs who are called Where and Wherefore. 'Where? Where?' asks one of them. 'Wherefore? Wherefore?' asks the other. Yes, they ask and ask, and the grownup sheep answer and answer. Where and Wherefore are allowed to ask about anything at all! And they get answers.

Today they tried to teach me how to wag my tail. Have you tried it? It's fun!
A hug from your son

MY DEAR BOY

How nice to hear that you are well, and that you are having a bit of fun at the high pasture. No, I have never tried wagging my tail. I have never been interested in foreign languages. But you can be sure they were great days up there in the high pasture when I was young! What a life! Roaming around freely on the meadow and into the woodland, seeking out everything green and juicy and simply gobbling it up. Towards autumn mushrooms popped up out of the ground and those who found a spot with good mushrooms went quite wild. Old cows were as frisky as calves. They flatly refused to go home again in the evening, because they wanted to find more, more! They were dotty! But generally, everything went on peacefully. We were lots of cows up there at that time. Cows from several farms were let loose together. We might happen to jab at each other and squabble, but mostly we were good friends. Every summer there were three dairymaids at Vikafjell, and they took such good care of us.

It was up there on the mountain that I learned to be fond of people. How splendid it was to stand close to a person who stroked and stroked over my belly and back, or scratched my head and spoke loving words to me. A dairymaid like that might be small and slender compared to us grown ones, but still she was like our mother, our bell cow whom we longed for and followed after. In the evenings those three dairymaids often sat on a hillock, humming and singing, and us cows gathered round to listen.

Yes, we had happy carefree days then, and the dairymaids boasted that the milk was so creamy and delicious that they had never known the like! And all the cheese and all the butter they made! No, now I am daydreaming. And it's a good thing! Pity you couldn't experience all that!
Love from Mother, dreamily

DEAR MOTHER

Do tell me more. But you are talking only about cows. Weren't there any calves there? And no bulls, I mean grownup bulls who only thought about one thing?
Love from Krollalfa

MY DEAR BOY

Yes, you may ask, and I can try to reply. It can't do any harm. There were a lot of calves, and they walked about freely like us grownups. That is to say rather, they ran. They often crowded together, running here and there. You may have heard the word 'calf-dance' or 'caper'? Yes, you tried it in the spring! Caper is when the calves jump and bound up and down slopes and hillocks. That's what they were up to, playing and fooling around and butting each other, and eating a little grass, or they went over to their mothers and sucked their fill. Yes, they were allowed to decide for themselves when they wanted to drink. Us cows didn't mind much if a strange calf came along and sneaked a drop for himself. We shared everything and were good friends in the same herd. And I can promise you that what our calves had was the real thing, and not a mixture of milk powder and water in a pail!

Ah, yes. The best day in the whole year was when we went up to the high pasture, and the heaviest was when we had to plod in a long, long line down again to the village early in the autumn. We simply followed the dairymaid right into the dark cowshed. No, first we spent a few weeks in the fields around the farm. We walked about there, waiting, but we never knew what awaited us, who would be taken away. Because you are quite right, it was the bull calves in particular they killed. And old cows, those who could no longer manage to fill the pail with milk. It's like this: people don't want to eat grass, but they are very hungry for meat. So, what are they to eat then?

Love from your mother, who has survived (up till now)

DEAR MOTHER

How good it is that you can tell me all this. I have longed to hear it. Longed for you to be honest with me. It feels so good that you are able to tell me about both what is good in life and what is bad. Then, I think particularly about the time of slaughter and death. You may believe it or not, but I feel more secure when I know you are thinking the same as me. Life is short and good, and nobody knows when you will become a chop.

Love from your son, who has survived up till now

DEAR SON

Yes, well now you know the same things as I do. I thought I wanted to spare you these heavy thoughts. You could simply eat and be comfortable until you were a little older, I thought. But that clever little brain of yours developed quickly. Now

you know what life is like, and what awaits us. We have to live with it. So now you can come home again to me, can't you? But promise me that you will never tell the other cows what I have said to you, about the final stinking fate of bull calves and old cows. And don't say it to me either. Don't remind me of what I have said. I want those bull calves of mine to be in peace. Do you understand? Are you coming?
Love from your mother

DEAR MOTHER

No, Mother, now that I know what life is like for those who live in the cowshed, in the hands of the farmer, I don't want that. I want to try something completely different. Maybe I'll suffer pain, and maybe I'll be hungry and cold. But anyway, I want to do it as a free bullock.

Inside the cowshed every day is the same. You stand there eating, you lie there ruminating, you shit into a gutter, you stare at the white wall. You dream, but only backwards in time. I want to dream forwards, and I want to dream about springtime! I know that there at home I would soon get a collar and chain around my neck, so that I would be standing stock still all winter. Out here I can move around freely, and I experience something new every day! Imagine that! I see the sun rise and set, I see the clouds scudding by or dropping rain down on me, the hillsides here are full of grass and many kinds of plants. I like white clover best, but the sheep are fond of it too, so we have to go looking for

that kind. The wild sheep have many tales to tell. They have travelled around so widely, but never been to Africa.
Love from your son, stuffed full of food

DEAR SON

Well, how nicely you tell about the life up there in the high pasture. It feels almost as if I were up there myself! I can see the clouds and feel the rain on my back, I taste the fresh flavour of white clover, I feel the evening sun which hardly warms my muzzle. Imagine, I could have been up there with you! I could have shown you a place where white clover and lady's mantle grow thickly! It is right down by the little stream which runs out of the high pasture, behind a huge rock. Think of me if you find that place! Chew the clover up and think of me!
A lick from your mother, Krollbrura!

GOOD MOTHER

I went there with my best friends, Where and Wherefore. 'Where are we going?' asked one. 'To look for a big rock,' I replied. 'Wherefore, wherefore?' asked the other. And after we had searched a little, here and there, we discovered the enormous rock and squeezed in behind it. Then there was nothing more to ask about, then it was just eating and being happy! Because you were right, clover and lady's mantle

grow very thickly there, and nobody has grazed there for a long time. We ate and ate all evening at the same little spot, and there was still more left for the next day. I kept thinking about you while I was eating, and nearly began to cry. You are a good mother!
A lick back from your good boy, Krollalfa!

DEAR SON

But when I was young, a wolf happened to come down from the high mountain and hunted us. That is to say, he hunted the sheep and the smallest calves, ones like you. He didn't dare to attack us grown ones. We just ran after him and chased him away. And I can promise you, he got a blow from the skull of one of us grown ones, then there wasn't a squeak left in him! But it was worse if there were several wolves in a pack. Then they gathered together around one of the weakest animals, and did not give up until the poor cow or calf was lying on the ground with the wolves all over it. I remember a gentle old cow who limped a little with her hind leg, wasn't she called Bliros? Yes well, the wolf noticed at once that it would be easy to get his teeth into Bliros and turn her over. How she screamed, lying there with the whole pack of wolves all over her! And her guts spilling out of her belly!

Yes, those were terrible times! The guts spilling out of her belly! Too terrible!

...No, I'm telling a lie. This thing with the wolves I have never experienced myself. It is only something my mother told me, and she had heard it from her mother. It isn't a tale for little children. But just relax! I don't think there are any wolves up in the mountains any more. We can thank the humans for that. You can just eat and be happy, safe in the clover meadow!

A hug from your mother

DEAR MOTHER

Oh, it isn't all that safe here either. The sheep tell me that once a huge bird came swooping down from the clouds. The sheep ran in all directions, but little Where remained standing there on the open plain wondering what was happening.

‘Where?’ he bleated.

Then he heard a great gusting sound and looked up. There came a bird with broad wings rushing straight towards him. The giant bird set its talons in his neck and tried to lift him. Where screamed as loudly as he could, and set off running towards the woodland, but the bird fought and struck with its wings, and tried to peck out his eye. In the end Where managed to get into some bushes, and that was how he was able to scrape the bird off him.

The grown sheep say it was an eagle, and we had better look out. But I am not afraid. I have grown a good deal in the past weeks, and my legs have become strong from climbing hillsides and rocks and running about on the pasture with all the lambs. I believe the eagle will not risk attacking me. But you should see what ugly scars Where has! And one of his eyes is white to this day! Maybe that is why he asks ‘Where?’ all the time. By the way, you have forgotten to tell me what the bulls did up here in the old days.
Happy son

DEAR SON

Yes, I had forgotten that, hadn’t I? The bulls were not allowed to come up to the high pasture with us. They were so wild and uncontrollable, after all. So they were never allowed to walk around freely, like us cows. But at home in the nearby field they walked about, inside a fence, by themselves. Cows by themselves and bulls by themselves. The bulls preferred scrapping and squabbling and butting each other. They obviously wanted to find out which was the strongest! Indeed, it could be exciting for us cows to watch the fights. It might take several days to determine, because there were always many young bulls wanting to test themselves against the old bull. The old cows cheered for the old bull, and we young cows cheered for the young ones. In the end they found out who the strongest was. It was either the old bull or one of the young ones. Then all the bulls were tired out. They had even forgotten to eat! Then they ate, and then they drank, and then they lay down to rest and chew the cud.

But that wasn't really what you wanted to know, if I know you. The bulls have something which we don't have, and we have something the bulls don't have. What we have, the bulls want, and what the bulls have, we want. You can find out the rest for yourself, you who are so clever.

Love from Mother

OH MOTHER!

No, you are being mean and old-fashioned now! Can't you simply say it as it is? I know you haven't tasted bull for several years. Do you suppose I haven't seen what goes on? I know that instead of the bull a man in a white coat comes and puts his fist inside you. Then it's done! That's how I began growing inside you. But what was it like when the bull came, wanting to have you?

Besides, every day I see what the wild sheep are up to. They do it several times a day. I ask why, and they say they can't stop. It is not enough for a sheep to eat and drink and

sleep and dream, they say. Every day I see what the rams have that the ewes don't have, and I see what the ewes have. And I know the smell. But what does it feel like? What does it feel like when you have desire to mate, and what does it feel like when the bull sticks that long red rod into you? You must be adult enough to be able to explain to me.
Love from a curious young person

OH YOU!

No, I don't want to tell you that. You just have to experience it for yourself, it can't be explained in words. I can only say that it is good, so good that I felt quite wild and crazy and could hardly stand still. But I had to, otherwise the bull couldn't get in, the fumbler! He was so heavy that my back creaked, and he rammed terribly, but it was so good that I would have given my life to be able to experience it once again. But now it's sure to be the veterinarian in autumn too.
Love from a disappointed mother

THANKS, MOTHER

Thanks for telling me that. I have become so big now that I have a right to know. And I think I know what you are talking about. It is something that tingles and explodes, isn't it? It is so good that it hurts. The rod stretches out under my belly, slippery and wet, it clamours here and there, begging to get into a certain place. But it can't. Never in my life.

That's the way it is. Both of us know that I will never be

able to experience what you told me about. I will never be able to mate. I will no doubt dream and wonder and long for heifers, but my rod will never be able to get in where it wants to. So why should I return to life in the closed-in cowshed? Can you tell me that? To stare at the heifers and cows which are standing tied up, each in her own stall? And then at last, one fine day, get to see the vet coming in the white coat to do the job I ought to have done? No thank you, I would rather long and dream out here in freedom!
Love from your son

DEAR SON

I understand you, you must not think otherwise. Do you suppose I don't long and dream as I stand here? Yes, I dream backwards, as you call it. What would we cows be thinking of, as we walked about staring at the bulls on the other side of the fence? Suddenly we would begin running about, and then we rode on each other as well as we could. There was a kind of giddy joy in that too. A bull is a bull and a cow is a cow, and never shall the two meet, I thought on my blackest days. But in spite of everything, I have tried it. I have had a taste of the real thing, as we say. So, I have these good memories to live on. I must be satisfied with that. It is painful and bitter, but such is my life. You are welcome to taunt me, saying I am regurgitating good memories and chewing the cud with them, chewing them again and again and swallowing them down once more. But it fills me up, that too.
A hug from Mother

DEAR MOTHER

But there is something else I have thought about a lot, and that is: Who is my father? I don't mean the vet, but the bull I am related to.
Your son

DEAR SON

No, I can't help you with that one. Nobody can be sure of such things these days. I myself haven't seen a bull for many years. Hardly any of the cows I have spoken to have seen hide or hair of a full-grown bull for many years. So how can I answer you? The only thing I can say is that he is the biggest and strongest and best bull there is. Because when he was young, he was chosen from among hundreds of other bull calves.

'This is a splendid young bull!' they said. 'He is so big and strong and broad-chested. He will be allowed to live!' they said. And you, my son, can be proud of that.
Love from Mother

OH MOTHER

Don't I have a right to know who my father is? I need to know! Where he lives and what he is called and what he looks like. At any rate tell me what colour his body is! Is he black or brown or white or spotted? Does he have great big horns?
Your son

DEAR ONE

Don't make a fuss now! I don't know anything. Nobody knows such things these days. The only thing you can do

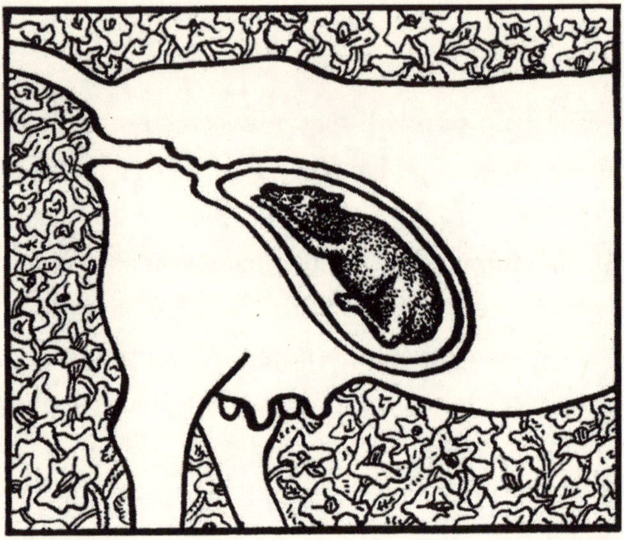

is look at your name. When you were born, the farmer gave you the name Krollalfa. And I have heard tell of a huge bull who is called Alfa.* So perhaps he is your father.
Love from Krollbrura

DEAR MOTHER

Thank you for telling me that! I am the son of Alfa and Krollbrura! Good to know! But where is he? What does he

* 'Alpha' or the first, most dominant, powerful leader of the pack.

look like? How *is* he, my father, the huge Alfa?
Love from Krollalfa

DEAR SON

You drive me dotty with your questions! I don't know where he is, or what he looks like. The only thing I can be sure of is that he lives like other full-grown bulls. There aren't many of them, as you know. But Alfa is allowed to live, and they take good care of Alfa. He gets the best possible food and drink. Apples and corn and turnips every day! He is so huge that he fills two ordinary stalls. But he is so strong that everyone is afraid of him. That is why they have put a ring through his nose. In through one nostril and out the other. They have fastened a strong rope to the ring, which they pull on. Can you imagine! The nose is certainly the most sensitive part of us.
Love from Mother

DEAR MOTHER

But calves won't come from that, will they?
Your son

DEAR SON

Don't you ever give up? Do you want to know absolutely everything I know? Listen up, then! Do you remember that talkative new cow who came here to the farm three years ago? Ringelihorn. She knew this, because she was a prize cow and had lived next door to a huge bull for several years. Well, she didn't get much joy of that bull anyhow. Because she didn't see hide or hair of him, only heard him bellowing and stamping on the floor. But then one day he had got so old that he was to be fetched by the slaughterhouse truck. Just before they were going to lead him out of the cowshed, she had a chance to talk to him. He stood there in the passage, waiting, so heavy and sad with the ring in his nose and a rope around each leg. Yes, he was an enormous slave, but the smell of bull was so raw and juicy that the poor cow was quite dizzy. And the bull must have felt the same. He looked at Ringelihorn and said he had been longing for her all his life.

'But you don't know me,' she said, making herself attractive.

'You are a living cow, aren't you?'

'Oh yes,' she replied, 'that is exactly what I am.'

'Yes, I can feel it in me, old as I am,' sighed the bull.

Then he told her how he had lived. Once a day they had led him into another room. There stood a cow so faithful and quietly ready, waiting. She was randy and mad, he knew that from her smell. And he climbed up on her with his front feet and mated. It was quickly over, and there was no more. The bull had finished and was led into his stall again. He was satisfied, at least for the first five years. But then he noticed that his beloved cow never turned around. Wasn't she interested in seeing what kind of bull came in at the door?

Why was he never allowed to lick her neck and muzzle? He called out to the cow, but she did not turn around. He tried to look into her eyes, but then he discovered that she was standing there so steadily without a neck or muzzle or eyes or ears. Yes, without a head at all! Not even a tail or hooves did she have!

Can you imagine, it was only a wooden cow with a cowskin over it! A fake cow with strong legs. Everything was fake. They even had false cow scent in a little bottle. They sprayed cow scent on the rear of the wooden cow, so that the bull was randy and willing and advanced. Then he climbed up onto the cow and gave his all. And the vet was satisfied. He thanked the bull and scurried out of the door with a full glass in his hands.

The false cow went on standing there, straddling her four legs. And the living cow, Ringelihorn, went on standing and straddling while the bull was led into the slaughterhouse truck. For the rest of her life, Ringelihorn spent every free minute dreaming that the bull climbed up onto her and mated so that the whole cowshed shook. It was good, but it was never more than a dream.

Love from your mother, exhausted from explaining

DEAR MOTHER

I wonder which of the two had the worst of it: the stupid bull or the false cow?

Love from your son

## DEAR UNHAPPY SON

What a question! You could have gone a long way, you too, I am sure! They are always on the lookout for promising bulls, and you are so broad across the chest and have such a good disposition. At least you had, before you ran away. Maybe you could have been a prize bull with descendants all over the country, just like your father. But you mustn't go up there and starve! And you must not, whatever happens, burrow down in sad thoughts. Surely you don't want your family to die out just because you look at everything darkly? No doubt *I* have descendants through all the heifers I have had, but it would have been nice if one of the bull calves too could leave a mark after himself and live on.

Dear son, comfort yourself with being related to the great bull Alfa and the beautiful Krollbrura, she who was once the prettiest young cow in the whole herd! No one gave as much milk as I! Do you realize that in my youth I received two prize rosettes at the big Cattle Show in Seljord? I could have got the first prize rosette as well, if it were not for my little defect. I don't know whether you noticed it, when you thrust yourself forward to suck? Yes, I have five teats. The fifth is mostly for show. I myself think it's simply charming. What do you say?

Your mother

DEAR MOTHER

Now you are going to hear something that the old ewe, Vera, told me. Yes, she likes telling stories about the old days, just as you do. And I understand more and more of the sheep language. Before I heard only bleating, but now I can distinguish the sounds from each other. Sheep are thoughtful animals. Do you know, once upon a time this one, Vera, was an ordinary sheep on a farm down in the village. You know the small farm which lies right by the waterfall. But then one fine day she ran away, just as I did! Yes really, it's quite true! She lived there on the farm in the company of seven cows and a horse and a flock of sheep and a farmer. And one day the vet came into the cowshed with the farmer. That vet was a cunning fellow. He was such a good ventriloquist. Yes, he could speak with his stomach, so that it sounded like the animal itself was talking.

'How is your life, you clever horse?' asked the vet.

'Thank you, toil and moil, grain to eat!' replied the horse.

Then the vet went over to one of the cows.

'How does he take care of you, you good cow?' asked the vet.

'Well, he pats and strokes, feeds and milks me!' replied the cow.

Then the vet went over to Vera, scratched her wool and asked:

'How about you, you pretty sheep, is he good to you?'

Then the farmer pushed in between them and whispered to Vera:

'If you say one word now, I'll kill you!'

Wasn't that a remarkable story? And so long! Vera can tell long stories like that. But I don't understand the end. Do you?

Your wondering son

DEAR SON

I understand this much, that it is no easier to be a sheep than a cow. But this is hardly a story to tell small children. Greet Vera from me and say that!

Your mother

DEAR MOTHER

But a few weeks later Vera ran away from the farmer and the farm and her flock of sheep. She couldn't stand life on the farm any longer. I said she was not to tell me such long stories, because Mamma had said so. But she just bleated and said she did as she pleased. It did children no harm to know what was ahead of them in life. Actually, she thinks the old ones tell us much too little about what they have experienced, and what they suppose and believe and think. We have to be honest with the young. That's what she said!

Your son, the one who ran away

MY DEAR BULLCALF

Now you must calm down! Don't let strange animals work you up against your own mother! There is more than one answer to such questions. Each cow and each ewe has to follow her own way and do what she believes is best for her own children.

A good mother

DEAR MOTHER

Okay now, relax! You have certainly done your best for both your heifer calves and bull calves. But I had to find out about this by myself. And now I have found out even more! I have something which the sheep don't have. I have the longest tongue in the world! One day Where and Wherefore asked me to put my tongue out as far as I could. And it was long, extremely long! They called out to the other sheep and they came running and stared and stared.

Proud son

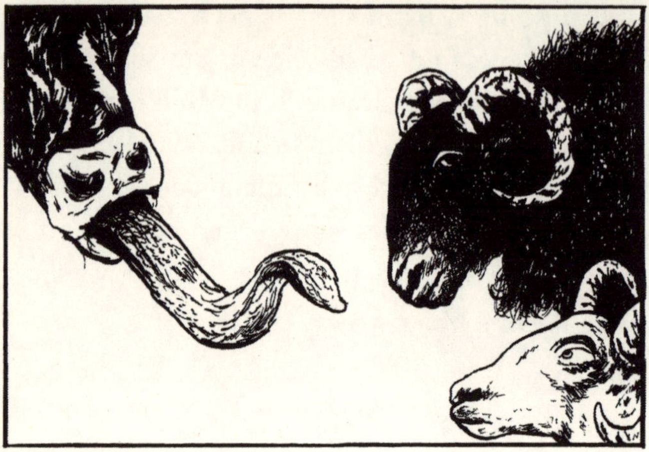

OH YUCK!

No, you must not shame yourself in front of strangers now! You must stop that sort of foolishness. It is well known that us cows and bulls have longer and stronger tongues than any other creatures. Longer than humans', longer than horses' or pigs' or sheep's and all animals one can think of. But is that anything to boast of? Is there something to standing and sticking out while others stare? You must stop believing you are so special. We all know the art of curling our tongues around grass and pulling it into us. Or licking far into our nostrils. So you are no champion in doing so. You won't get a prize for such foolishness!
Mother

ONCE AGAIN YUCK

Have you thought of replying? Have you stopped that disgusting tongue-fooling yet?
Mother

DEAR MOTHER

Yes, you have indeed been waiting for an answer. But all of yesterday I wasn't able to send you so much as a single word. Why? Because one of my writing feet got stuck between R and T. I tried to wriggle it, but the foot stuck fast, just like a stick in dried cowshit. So I sat there staring at these letters. RT. The letters sit so close together, one wouldn't think it was intended for us to use them for anything at all.
Your son

MY LITTLE CLEVERCLOGS

You are right. We are created to live close together and lick each other and wander about in a herd as much as we like. Yes, that is what we use our feet and tongues for. But these days it has become so crazy that we have to speak up to make contact. How long can we stand tightly tied up in our own stalls before we are destroyed and lose the ability to socialize with other animals? When the whole world is about rattling chains and food in at one end and shit out of the other and milk out of the udder. Yes indeed, it is said that necessity teaches the solitary cow to speak, but we go astray with words alone. It is like going out of one's own body and not finding the way home again. We are cows of flesh and blood, after all, and words are only like foam and bubbles of air on top of the milk pail. Blow on that foam and it goes to nothing.

Good that you got your foot free again! You must be careful not to damage the letters! Because then it would be completely over between us. Then how would we talk to each other? You are the dearest one I have!
Your mother

DEAR MOTHER

Okay! I know that I should only press lightly down with the tip of my hoof when I type. But when I get carried away, I crash down with all my might. Yes, my front feet go by themselves, and the words swarm out almost before I get to think them. It is like running mindlessly, ecstatically, over green meadows. It is fun. It is fun writing under stress. And even more fun to know that you can read these words and understand how I am getting on. A word is a wonder, have you thought of that?
The son in freedom

DEAR SON

Yes, I have thought about it a lot. It is unbelievable that these letters can bring out the taste of clover and green meadows and frisking calves. Yes, even the great bull himself. I just say the words 'great bull' and he comes striding along blowing through his nostrils. Do I know what he wants this time? I don't need to tell you that again. But it is good.

Really, since we have become blessed with letters and words, we just have to take care to use them as well as we can. Everything dies. Livestock die, relatives die, as the old ones say, but I know something that never dies.

Your mother in the stall

DEAR MOTHER

What's that then?

DEAR SON

The word, I reply, but then I am talking above my head. The reputation of a good cow, that lives. Who knows? Perhaps something extraordinary is going to happen, after they have chopped me limb from limb and turned this poor carcass over into bull-beefsteak and mincemeat, and one or another meat-hungry two-foot sits there chomping me into himself, then these words might seep through from his intestines and into his way of thinking.

'Who is talking?' he asks then. But he can't know that.

'I feel so calm,' he mumbles, 'could it be something in the meat?'

'Yes, there is always something in the meat,' comes the reply, as if deep inside him.

DEAR MOTHER

The bit about mince I understand, but how could you become bull-beefsteak?

DEAR SON

I am ashamed to tell you such a thing, but just the same I will. Why? Now I remember something two of my fellow-calves shouted to each other once when they were standing on the edge of a steep cliff by the river, above the pool we call Svartkulp. They stood there, trembling, ready to throw themselves over the cliff and down into the black water.

'If you dare, I dare too!' they egged each other on. Yes, dear son, you dare, and I am willing to believe you are my relative and have this daring courage from your mother's side. If you dare speak out, I dare too. If you dare think about death, I dare too. Perhaps you will never get as far as having a taste of a graspable heifer. So allow yourself then, in the name of the Heavenly Cow, to taste it in dreams!
Your mother forever

MOTHER

I don't want to dream away my life. I want to live here and now. But nothing happens here. I am sick with longing.
Your son

OH, YOU DEAR ONE!

Poor calf, having to wander about alone like that, suffering. Here in the cowshed there is always something going on, and you know the way home. Now Ringelihorn has thought up something new. You know she is full of ideas and stories. It's the result of her getting to see so much of the world before she came here to us. Suddenly she is standing gazing unblinkingly into a cowpat. She stands gazing for ever so long.

'What's up with you?' we others ask.

'I see so much strange,' she replies, 'and now I can see into the future!'

Well, she says she can see the future in a cowpat! None of us believe a word of it, but everyone lets out fresh cowpats and wants to know the latest news about the future. Then Ringelihorn stands gazing fixedly into one or another's future. The first evening she foretold that Moonshine would have triplets. She will have three absolutely identical heifer calves, and her descendants will be as numerous as the flies on the cowshed wall on a summer day. What a joy! Yes, you should have been there and done your duty!

Your mother

OH MOTHER!

But this is just bullshit, Mother. Don't believe in nonsense like that. Ringelihorn is only trying to give herself airs.
Your son

OH YOU!

Do you think I'm stupid? Truly, one who can tell the future has great power. That showed itself the following evening. Because then Ringelihorn foretold that another heifer, the big, beautiful Plomma, would have a worse fate. She would have a water-calf floating along in the gutter, but no living calf. You know, a water-calf is only a thin membrane and running water, without feet or body or mouth or tongue. The farmer and his wife would stand there, searching and wondering what had happened to the actual calf, the flesh and blood calf. But it would not come. Plomma was to get a wretched water-calf like that three times. As soon as Ringelihorn had said that, we all knew that a heifer like that

would not live. Poor Plomma had received a death sentence! Because every cow who does not bear a calf will be sent away and slaughtered. Plomma stood there shaking her head and rattling her chain. What did she have to face? Well, the next day she tried to gloss over her future, with all sorts of ingenious nonsensical rubbish. But Ringelihorn stuck to her guns, she wasn't fooled. A water-calf it was, and a water-calf it would be! Three of them, even!
Your mother

## OH MOTHER!

As I said, it's nothing but bullshit. I hope Plomma will have three fine heifer calves, and that Ringelihorn gets a huge water-calf to drown herself in.
Your son, bored of nonsense

## MY SON

When it was my turn to have my fortune told, Ringelihorn could tell that in the spring I would meet a tall dark bull! I, in my old age! Well, what great luck! I see the bull in front of me, rolling my eyes. But that isn't all. Because she woke up in the night and alleged that she had once examined one of your pats. And that pat was something unique, oval and full of nooks and crannies, and with a little extra bit that lay by itself. You couldn't even stand still when you shat, I suppose.

'My dear Ringelihorn, what did you discover?' I asked, shocked and scared.

'I saw that Krollalfa, your son, would set out on a long, long journey. He would encounter many kinds of difficulties on his way. He would be cold and hungry and fight wild animals. And in the end, he would meet a big, strange cow. That strange cow would be what he was searching for.

After that I couldn't get to sleep. I keep thinking about it. What am I to believe?
Your mother

OH MOTHER

You shouldn't believe in cowpats, at any rate! You know very well that no two pats are alike. So how can your future be revealed in every single pat? Do you have hundreds of futures to expect? Idiot!
Your son

DEAR SON

Don't take that tone! What do you have to offer me? Don't you understand anything about what it is like to be a mother? Once a mother, always a mother! I feel so lonely, standing here. I won't have any more calves, I know. You were the last. What would be next then?

Every day I expect something good to happen to me, but I don't know what it will be. Ah yes, now I know! A tall dark bull would change my whole life. Imagine something so marvelous happening to me in my old age! I squeeze my eyes shut, and there he comes striding, wide-legged and wild, so randy that the rut steams off him.

'But can't you see how slack and sway-backed I have become? I'm ashamed of you seeing me like this. My joints are sticking out, my udder sags. You should have come to me in my loveliest youth!'

'It's the inside that counts,' he says and climbs up onto me from behind.

OH MOTHER

From behind? Mamma mia! How else would he climb up?

DEAR SON

Do you really have to split hairs about my dreams? Can't you help me dream instead? Imagine it's the great bull Alfa himself, standing in the cowshed passage one fine day, bellowing? Your father.
Your mother, dreaming

DEAR MOTHER

Yes, of course! Of course the great bull Alfa. Otherwise it's the slaughterer who hasn't finished his job.
Your son

DEAR SON

Yes, well it *is* your father! Big and black as a winter night, and so broad that he shatters the doorframes on his way in to me. But he hardly notices all that, he just charges ahead, and the floor shakes at every step he takes. Then he is standing just behind me, bellowing, stretching out his neck and curling his upper lip. His voice makes the windowpanes clatter, the flies tumble down from the ceiling and flop onto the floor, the cobwebs are torn to shreds.

'What do you want?' I ask in a trembling voice.

'Are you really asking about that? Don't put on an act!'

He must be able to see that the mucus is running out of me, and that I am ready.

'How is Krollalfa, my son?' he asks suddenly.

'Oh, he's on a walk up in the woods just now, but he'll soon be home,' I reply.

'That's a pity. I thought he would enjoy seeing how it should be done. What is to be done now. But I can't wait any longer.'

Then he advances. He sniffs, blowing hot air at my precious parts, and it is so good that I am almost fainting, his breath is so hot, and I am so randy.

'Oh come, just come!' I shout, standing as wide-legged and steady as I can.

Then he leaps up on top of me so all my joints crack. But I stand there. I stand, I quiver, and he thrusts in. Yes, he thrusts and thrusts, and I take all he has.
Your mother, in a wet dream

DEAR SON

What is it with you? Aren't you going to reply? Surely you can tolerate your mother dreaming herself away? I only meant I didn't need you spoiling my good dreams. But I do need you to say you understand how I feel! My dear little

calf, you aren't jealous, are you? You are in my dream too! Answer me now!
Lonely again

DEAR MOTHER

But this mating thing, is it never satisfied?
Love from he who asks

DEAR SON

It is like eating. You are good and full, but then you get hungry again. And now you know what hunger is like. It is impossible to resist. You know, it's the same way for all animals. We are not embarrassed by each other, we sniff ahead and do as we must. Only the bodies of people are such that they have to dress up. But over the years I have seen a bit of everything when they finally undo their clothes and can't control themselves any longer. Both here in the cowshed and out in the woods. Then they are most like cows and bulls.
Love from she who has seen a bit of everything

DEAR MOTHER

Then they must know how we feel? Do people know that? That we need to go about freely and sniff each other and mate when the need arises?
Curious, black

DEAR SON

Yes, the body has its needs, they know that. Everyone knows it. I have told you about the rutting season. When randiness overcame us, we forgot both grass and rest times. We simply ran after each other, with wild glances and tails high in the air. At that time, we had a cow in the herd who always had to whine and complain. She was called Valborg, and she was a grumpy, bad-tempered cow all her life. She said it was wrong and shameful that we cows rode on each other. The Heavenly Cow would punish us for such sick behaviour, she alleged. But do you suppose that Valborg herself didn't go and lick young heifers in a certain place when nobody saw it?

Yes, well, she went away a long time ago. She has passed away, as we old ones say. Or she was slaughtered and flayed and butchered and eaten up, as you would put it, and peace be with her. Now she must be lying at the right forefoot of the Heavenly Cow, looking down at me and criticizing me for each word I say to you. No, I am being nasty now! Forget it! The Heavenly Cow does not allow herself to be fooled.

Your mother, who doubts everything now and then

DEAR MOTHER

Today something unbelievable happened up here! A dairymaid came to the high pasture! Or at least a young woman, or a girl, I can't be sure. She has a thick plait down her back, almost like a cow's tail. At first, I was scared, no, worse than that. I was terrified! She called out to me, and she called to the wild sheep. They ran all over the place. They are completely wild, after all. They've never been near humans and never inside a building.

But that girl did not give up. She called in her soft voice with a wisp of sorrel in her hand. I sneaked away, because sorrel isn't anything to wish for. But she followed after me. She was coming to catch me! What should I do?

I felt so strange inside when I heard the human voice and smelled her scent. Had she come to catch me and drag me down to the village again? No, that didn't make sense. Because she laughed so loudly and in waves when she discovered me standing stuffing in the rest of the white clover. As if she couldn't believe her own eyes. Do you suppose she is a dairymaid who has been hibernating in one of the buildings? One who has been dead and then come alive again? A ghost like you and the old cows talk about late at night?

Love from your son

DEAR SON

Well, it does sound peculiar. Are you sure it's a plait she has, of human hair, and not a cow's tail sticking out under her skirt? Shove your nose in there and you'll smell cow scent. Then it's a wood nymph. But do it quickly, before she gets up to any mischief!

Love from a seriously worried Mother

DEAR MOTHER

Take it easy! She is not wearing a skirt. I thought I ought to do as you said. But when she turned up early this morning, she sat down on a stone and loosened her plait. It was sunny and her hair shone. Then she went over to the stream, bent down and washed her hair. She knelt with her head in the stream, blowing bubbles! Then she dried her hair and brushed it. Now it is hanging loose down her back. It has waves and looks more like a meadow than the rear end of a cow. Her hair smells at least as nice as the back of a cow. But quite different. It smells more like red clover, as sweet as a warm summer day. So, I think you can rest easy. At any rate, I am doing so.

Happy son

DEAR ONE

Pull yourself together! Fairy folk can change their shape and entice you in all sorts of ways! She'll catch you suddenly! She often uses a fine herd of gorgeously plump fairy cows as a means of enticement. But if you follow the herd into the mountain, you see that it is only skin and bone. The only food they get is time passing. Yes, they eat their own meagre days of life.

Frightened Mother

## OH NO, MOTHER!

Yes, she coaxes, but only with good things. All of a sudden, this girl has become my very best friend. She scratches my head and feels whether I am soon getting horns. She pats and strokes along my sides and says nice words to me. All at once she finds a tick sitting and sucking blood out of me. Then she says, 'You poor thing', and doesn't stop until she has picked me clean again. So you can say that life up here is good now, nearly as good as in the good old days of yours, with animals and a human enjoying themselves in free and peaceful nature. Even though I miss you and the other cows and specially the calves. Especially that big one with a white moon on her forehead. Moonshine. The one who is going to have triplets.

A hug from your son

## DEAR SON

Well, look at that. That girl has become your very best friend! That's how quickly it happens. A few kind words and a little patting and stroking. You who scorned me for being fond of the farmer and his wife and their children! Now you can feel it in your body. We need each other, cows and humans, you see!

Mother

OH MOTHER

Don't tease me! I need her because I have nobody else. It is you and the other cows and calves I need the most!
Your son

DEAR SON

Yes, forgive me! I was cheeky to you. But it is odd, what you tell me about that girl. I have heard of people who just wander around in nature and do nothing, but I have never met anyone like that myself. So, you are lucky. What does she do all day? Does she have food with her? What is she? Where does she sleep? Is she good at caring for animals, do you think? Do you think she can milk? I mean, do you think she can cut grass and dry it into hay, so you'll have something to chew on? Yes, maybe she can collect so much that you will be able to manage through the winter?
Love from Mother

DEAR MOTHER

She has a way with animals anyway. The wild sheep come closer and closer. Where and Wherefore have been right up to her feet with their muzzles. She sits on a stone and sings, and then they become so curious that they can't move.

But I am the one who keeps closest to her. I am allowed to suck her fingers as much as I like. But I must be careful and not get too eager, because then my teeth sink into her fingers and she screams loudly and scolds me. I often lie

with my head in her lap, sucking while she sings. She sings, now and then, like the children at home on the farm sang for us little calves in the calf pen.
Love from your good son

MY DEAR CHILD

Imagine if I could have been up there with you! I would have shown you more good grazing grounds in between the little woodlands. If only I could get to smell the fresh mountain air and taste the sweet clover just once more in my life! If only I could have met a strong bull up there in the forest. And then called home again in the evening by a kind dairymaid and scratched on my back. One who would have taken the time to speak kindly to me and sing for me! Perhaps she could have milked me with her hands too, in the old way. How easily I would have let the milk out of my udder then! Far from the closed-in cowshed and the sucking milk machine which isn't able to say an intelligent word. Oh, my goodness! How you can make me long and dream!
Love from Mamma

MY DEAR SON

What has happened? Now I haven't heard from you for several days. You haven't forgotten me, have you? No, I can't believe that. But are you ill? Have you injured yourself? You can't have got yourself stuck between the letters again. Has the pack of wolves turned up again? No, oh no! You can't

have gone astray into the olden days, so that both the wood nymph and the pack of wolves and all sorts of ghosts have come creeping out and caught you? You aren't lying there with your guts out of your belly, are you? Answer me, then! I can't sleep!
Your only Mother

NO, OH NO, MY BOY

Now you must give me an answer, or I will lose both my milk and my voice! I see you before me lying in the scree with a broken leg! Oh, how you complain, oh how piteously you call out! But there is nobody to help you. And soon the eagle will come and peck at you. No, oh no, no!
Your Mother, completely insane

DEAR MOTHER

No, the wolves haven't turned up. Something much worse has happened. One morning I was standing as usual outside the little house, waiting for my girl to wake up and come out to me. But she didn't wake up. She didn't come out. I didn't dare go away from there, because I was afraid she would be lost to me. I bellowed and mooed, but nothing happened. All the wild sheep began drifting further and further away from the pasture.

'Wherefore should we wait here?' asked Wherefore. Then he went into the little wood with the others. At last I couldn't see the sheep anymore. I mooed, but nobody replied. And my moos were so sad that I was about to cry. I tried to comfort myself by eating a bit of the grass around the house, but there was nothing else to eat there. I stood there with a few withered stalks in my mouth and wept.

What had happened? Surely she couldn't just go away like that, without saying goodbye? Then I noticed that the door into one of the buildings was ajar. I butted the door and squeezed in.

It smelled of dead flies and mice and humans. Oh, there was the good smell of the girl with the lovely hair, and I mooed so happily. But nobody replied, nobody stirred.

I stood for a long time, simply sniffing. Then I lay down on the floor and waited. I waited and waited until I was completely frozen stiff and my stomach screamed for food. Then I got up and went out again. Now I have been walking around the houses here on the high pasture, waiting, for two days, but she whom I had become so fond of has just gone away from me. Far away. I am quite alone. How could she think of such a thing, she who was so fond of me? She couldn't just walk away, could she?
Love from your son

DEAR SON

What has happened, I could have told you about in advance, if you had asked. She has gone home to her own, you must understand. She was a human who had to go home again to humans. She couldn't manage without them. Because she is just like other living beings. Each and every one wants to be with their own kind. That's how it is with humans, and that's how it is with animals, my boy. You must notice it yourself, as you go around grazing with the flock of sheep. Have you found them again? I hope so, then you won't be completely alone. But one fine day they too will disappear. Sheep are fine animals, but they are not like cattle. You are longing, aren't you? Even though you have the company of sheep? Don't you feel that you are longing for another smell, for another voice? Yes. I believe you are longing for the smell of cows and calves and for me, your mother. We are waiting for you here at home, all of us. I must greet you so warmly from Fagros, Dagros and little Moonshine. She who was born on the same day as you. Moonshine has become a big calf now. Soon a heifer and ready to bear a calf. With strong legs and a shining hide, and with a white moon on her forehead.

A hug from your own Mamma

DEAR MOTHER

Fortunately, I found the flock of sheep again. So, you can just stand there in the cowshed in company with the other cows and be satisfied with life. It is no use coaxing me with smells and warmth and enough to eat. Or Moonshine with the shining hide. Because I have had a taste of what it is to be a free calf. I'm going to stay up here. But what are you going to eat in the winter? you ask. Right, I can tell you that. When I was inside the little house looking for my girl, I found a huge pile of hay on the floor. I believe that was where she had slept. She had hidden herself in the hay so she wouldn't be cold. Now I go in there and eat a little every day, without the others noticing. I try to save it, because I know that the winter is long. But it is not so easy when you are hungry and the hay is lying right in front of you. It smells good, yes, the hay smells of high summer, even though it is old. Thin, fine stalks, both of grass and a good deal of clover. I even find a little lady's mantle here and there!

The sheep believe I go into the house every day to look for my dairymaid, as they call her.

'Where are you going?' asks Where.

'Into that grey hut over there,' I reply.

'Wherefore, wherefore?' asks Wherefore.

'I can't be bothered to answer that anymore,' I reply.

So I get out of lying that time. I go in through the door and sniff the air indoors. The smell of the girl has completely disappeared, but the hay smells good. Then I stand there eating old hay until I am almost full. After a while I go out to the others and nibble at the remains of the green grass. They don't notice anything.

Love from me

DEAR SON

Oh, how pleased I am that you have found that bundle of hay! Now you have only to use it sparingly, because it is true

and well known that winter is long. And whatever happens you must not let the others realize what you have found. You are bigger than them and need more food, and I so much want to have you back alive, so I can look you in the eyes and lick you, my own unruly son. Live well up there!
Warm love from Mother

DEAR MOTHER

It is bitingly cold now. Today we had to scrape away a thin layer of snow to reach down to the grass and moss. But it's okay, this too. The sheep know how to do it, and I am learning! The cold bites my muzzle, but I have grown a slightly thicker fur. Not like sheep's wool, but it helps anyway. I believe it will be alright.

Yes, I'm not shrinking from winter! Let it come, large and white and long and biting. I'm sure I'll manage to slog right through it and come out again on the other side!

But now I have something new to tell you. Recently my skull itched so. It itched and itched, and do you know what? I am getting horns! Small, rock-hard, white horns! They aren't very big yet, but I think they will be fine! Inherited from my father! How do I know my horns are white? Every day I play-fight with Where and Wherefore, and they said so. But I am too strong for them. I simply shove them here and there and toss them head over heels until they are on their knees, bleating.
A hug from your strong son

DEAR SON

Nice to hear that you are so fit and well! To think that you have got both fur and horns! But you must be careful and look after yourself anyway. You are not to imagine that you are an outdoor animal for that reason. I am proud of you and would so much like to see you now. But I am afraid for you too. You are young and don't know much about life.
A hug from Mother

MOTHER!

All day yesterday Where and Wherefore stood nibbling at me. Why? Well, they wanted to nibble my ear-tags off. Those yellow tags should be removed! Where and Wherefore nibbled and nibbled, and it hurt. But in the end the tags fell off, one after the other. And I thought: Now I am free. Absolutely free! Nobody owns me. I ran all by myself high up the hillside to get the feel of it. I was so happy! Though it stung and bled. But I was so happy.
Free calf

DEAR ONE

You make me uncomfortable. My poor calf, all you have to go through because of those crazy dreams of yours.
Love from Mother

DEAR MOTHER

What am I to do? Now there is hardly a blade of grass left here at the high pasture. Each day the flock of sheep drift further and further away to find something to chew on. I go with them, but in the evenings they don't bother to go home to the high pasture. Of course, I would rather go home at night, so I can curl up in the sheep shed. It's warmer there, especially when we huddle close together. Then we are out of the wind, and we are sheltered from rain or snow falling on us. But the sheep don't bother about such things. They keep warm anyway. Well, what am I to do?
Your son on the mountain

DEAR SON

I think you know the answer. The time of slaughter is over for this year, and you can safely come home again. The farmer is sure to give you a good welcome, I am certain of it. The other bull calves have gone, and it has become so empty and quiet in the cowshed. You should have seen old Fagerlin, how pleased she was when she was led outside. Right up to the end she believed she was going out on a long and blessed journey, perhaps all the way to the Cattle Show in Seljord.

Imagine, she believed that, even though she had been plagued with mastitis for years. She was a big milker, but it was a great strain on the udder to make so much milk. She was red and swollen week after week, and the milk simply had to be thrown away. I can't count how many times the vet came in and injected her. In the end she was three-teated. Not a drop of milk came out of the fourth teat. She ought to have known then that her days were numbered. Three-teated, that's a death sentence. But Fagerlin refused to believe it. Cattle

Show indeed! Oh well, she was a brave cow who fooled herself and kept up her courage to the last. It's a strain to be a big milker. We are not made to make more milk than our own calf needs to grow and fatten up. But we have to keep going for the humans' sake. Each one who doesn't milk the

pail full, will be slaughtered and used for humans' food. So they have us in their clutches, no matter what.
Your mother says it as it is

DEAR MOTHER

Yes, I know. But how does it help? And what are you getting at?
Cold son

DEAR OBSTINATE BILLYGOAT

What I am getting at is, that we mustn't forget that humans have feelings too. Almost like other animals. Come home and live for a while longer with me! Remember that the farmer spared me, even though I give much less milk than before. Yes, less than any of the others. In fact, I am the eldest now. Perhaps he spared me because I was his wife's pet cow. She often came out into the cowshed late in the evening. She stood there stroking my neck, resting her head against my belly, just like a dairymaid in the old days. She would stand like that for a long time without saying a word, and sometimes she used to speak in such a sad tone of voice. You know, don't you, that there are only two kinds of animals that can cry tears? That is cows and humans. I have never seen bulls or men crying, so they can't have the ability. Once she suddenly came to me, early one morning, long before milking time, dressed up for town, elegant. Then she said goodbye and went away. But I could never forget her tears and the good scent she had on her. A flowery meadow, in the middle of winter! Humans are so powerful that sometimes I wonder how much power the Heavenly Cow actually has. Enough of that! The farmer's wife took the children with her and went away from me and from her husband and the whole farm. Even though she had been so lucky to have her bull all to herself for so many years.

The first weeks after she had gone, he came out into the cowshed instead. It was I he came to, perhaps to seek comfort. But he wasn't one to allow cows close to him. No, he could neither laugh nor cry nor speak out. He did not put his arms around me even once. Poor fellow. He just stood there twisting the udder cloth and sighing. I couldn't help him.

Your loving mother

DEAR MOTHER

And you can't help me. I don't want to turn back, I don't want to come sneaking home again!

Ice-cold son

DEAR LOST SON

What shall I say? I am as helpless as you. But at least I can tell you that I was young and silly once, I too. When I had my first calf, I was as happy and proud as only a cow can be. Because I was no longer a heifer, I was a proper cow! I felt exactly like a heavenly cow! My dear little calf was so strong and lovely and good at sucking. The calf got on his feet as soon as I had licked him clean. A beautiful little calf he was, and almost completely white. Like milk. But then the farmer came and took him away from me! I didn't understand anything. How could they think of such a thing?

The calf stood in a pen at the other end of the cowshed, complaining bitterly. My udder was brimming with milk. Each time the calf complained, the milk began to drip and run by itself. Straight down onto the floor the milk ran. What could I do?

Then they came and put a milking machine in place under me. The machine sucked, and I tried to speak to it, as I had done to my calf.

'Drink, my calf, it's good for you,' I said and it drank.

'Oh, today you were greedily hungry!' I said.

And when the milking machine let go of my teats, I asked:

'Are you nice and full now, my child? Or would you like to have a little more? I think there's a little drop left!'

Yes, I was so young and silly at that time. But the following day I understood what was going on, and from then on, I didn't say a word to the milking machine. No, I didn't let myself be fooled twice, however much it made a smacking sound, fawning and sucking.

Love from your mother

DEAR MOTHER

'What are you up to?' ask the sheep.

I don't know what to reply. The sheep say I have got the sheep stare, and it must be very serious, as serious as the goat cough. But it isn't true, I haven't got the sheep stare. Though I have discovered something funny. When it snows, I like to stand gazing up at the sky. I gaze up between the snowflakes. Then it feels as if all of me is floating in thin air! I climb and climb, higher and higher, until I feel I am a heavenly cow. Then I don't feel cold any more, I just fly upwards! But as soon as I look towards the sheep or the woods, the trip ends, and I am down on earth again.
Love from a son of the earth

DEAR SON

Yes, I didn't tell you much about the Heavenly Cow before you left. The Heavenly Cow is so big that she fills the whole sky. The dome of the sky itself is her belly! Do you know how broad she is between the horns? The horns are so long that they reach from night and far into the daytime. The moon is the shining button on one horn, and the sun is the button on the other horn. She is that big! But now and then the Heavenly Cow changes herself into a quite ordinary cow. Then she comes down onto the earth. She tastes the grass and drinks the water in the rivers to see if it is fresh and clean. Then she looks for a herd of ordinary cows and goes in among them. She moos and keeps company with them. In the evening the mighty Heavenly Cow goes into an ordinary stall and gets a chain around her neck! Of course, the farmer doesn't realize anything.

'Who in the world is this cow?' he asks.

But that he can never discover. Because the Heavenly Cow has no tags in her ears, nobody owns the Heavenly Cow.

Outside the cowshed people stand gazing up at the sky, understanding nothing. Because the sun and the moon have gone! Those poor human creatures believe the whole world is coming to an end. But the next day, when the farmer comes out to the cowshed to take the muck out and milk, the new cow has gone too. The chain is there, dangling. The cowshed door is closed, but the cow has disappeared without a trace.

'Where in the world is my new cow?' he asks.

Oh, the sun has come up again anyway, shining so brightly in through the cowshed window, and in the evening the moon comes out. Then we cows know that the Heavenly Cow is in her place, gazing down at the earth. She is watching over us. But humans will never be able to understand this.

Love from your mother, who doesn't understand everything either

DEAR MOTHER

'Now, you have the sheep stare for sure!' say the sheep. Because I look upwards even when it isn't snowing. Then I gaze at the moon. I think about what you told me about the Heavenly Cow. How has she reached her place up in the sky again? Maybe she has done as I do, gazed up between the snowflakes until she became light? Tell me more, Mother!

Curious son

I don't know much more. But I'll tell you what my mother told me before we were separated. Once, a long time ago, the earth was barren and empty. There was nothing but grass and forests and water. There was not so much as a bird or a fly. The Heavenly Cow hung up there on high, peering down on all that greenery.

No, it's too bad to have all that fine grass, she thought. Then she called to the huge bull which lives in the darkness under the earth's crust. The red-hot Earth Bull is made of fire and molten rock. He pushed his way up through the earth's crust, roaring and thundering. Trailing flames and smoke he strode up to the Heavenly Cow and mated until the entire empty world trembled and shook. Then he dug his way down again into the glowing embers.

When the time was ripe, the Heavenly Cow gave birth to two fine calves, and licked them and laid them in a manger.

The Heavenly Cow had so much milk that it streamed out over the Milky Way and dripped down onto the earth, and the calves drank the heavenly milk. Then they bounded out of the manger and ran and capered away over the meadows. There they mated with each other, and new calves arrived. In the end there was an enormous herd which roamed around and ate the juicy grass. They let out wet cowpats everywhere, and out of these cowpats all living things came crawling out. First the flies, then the worms, then humans and in the end the birds. Yes, on the third day the first humans crawled out of cowpats.

Well, you may believe what you like, but I want to tell you the rest. My mother said that one day it will begin raining milk from the sky again, and then the Heavenly Cow will be on her way back to the earth. Teat-warm milk will fall like rain over fields and meadows, over animals and humans, and all living beings will stick out their tongues and drink their fill of the heavenly milk. But it won't be merely a joke when the Heavenly Cow comes. Because then all cows and calves and bulls will be set free. From that day we will be able to wander freely around in green, juicy meadows, and all humans who have been cruel to us will be put into stalls and get chains around their necks. That's the way it is.
Love from Mother

DEAR MOTHER

You tell it so well, but I don't know what to believe. I would really like to have a little of that heavenly milk now.

I stick my tongue out, but the rain falling down is white, ice-cold snowflakes. I am afraid it will be too long for me to wait for the Heavenly Cow to come back. It's getting colder every day, and the hay is running out fast. I don't know whether I believe in spring.
Love from your cold calf

DEAR SAD BOY

Spring will come, that is for sure. You have so many dark thoughts, and I don't understand where you get them from. In any case, they are not from me, because I have always been bright and light-hearted.

But now I recall something funny that happened when I was younger, when I was the bell cow. Yes, as you know, I had the honour of being the bell cow the last two summers we went up to the high pasture. The old cow had to stay behind at home and take it easy when the day came to leave for the high pasture, and with that she was out of the picture. I had given birth in the spring just like her, and went around the whole summer with a bursting udder. So the dairymaid knew that I wanted to go home to the pasture every evening to avoid more milk leaking out. Oh, what a day, when I was given the collar around my neck and the splendid bell which rang and sang so sweetly! Then I set off with the other cows after me. But we had not gone far before a cow came up beside me and wanted to get past. That was Valborg, and she was jealous, you know! She tried again and again. In the end I shoved her into the stream, and then she had to stay quietly behind.

But when we reached the pasture and were to be milked, it was the same fuss. The dairymaid came with her pail and wanted to milk me first, as was only fair. But that obstinate Valborg came and pushed past me. Then I gave her such a fierce jab that she sank to her knees. That was how it had to be! Then the dairymaid milked me and the other cows in turn. Only one cow was left. But by then Valborg was so sulky that she dodged away. She went further and further away from the pasture. What were they to do with a cow who didn't know what was for her own good? Well, all three dairymaids got together to catch her, so she could be milked before dark. But then she waded out into the water and stood with her udder underwater, so nobody could reach it! Yes, she was a stubborn beast. They coaxed her with salt, and they coaxed her with flour, but Valborg was adamant. She did not get on land again until the dairymaids had gone to bed. Next morning the dairymaid came and wanted to milk Valborg first. That was how she got her own way. But I wasn't going to stand for that!

Of course, I had to insist on my right to be milked first. So, I simply kicked the pail over. Otherwise I wouldn't have been respected as bell cow. Do you understand me?
Former Bell Cow

DEAR MOTHER

The sheep don't believe in the Heavenly Cow. They only bleated when I told them how everything was created. I told them that the sheep were created first, just after the cows. But it didn't help. They refused to believe that the first sheep had crawled out of a cowpat.
Your son

DEAR SON

Let the sheep believe whatever they like! The Heavenly Cow has helped us so many times. And you surely don't believe that it is a sheep running the whole world?
Mother

HELP ME, MOTHER

Now everything is ruined! Where asked what I was going to do, and I replied that I was going into the grey hut for a bit. Then Wherefore asked why, and I replied as usual that I wanted to go in to sniff the smell of the dairymaid who used to live there. Then I went. But do you suppose they didn't sneak after me! Sheep are curious animals too, so I ought to have thought of that. But I didn't think, because I was so hungry and cold as I stood there eating for dear life. I ate with my eyes closed, so that I could dream about the girl and the summer at the same time. Oh, it was so vivid! I smelled the scent of summer grass and heard the girl pottering about behind me. But when I turned around to look,

Where and Wherefore were standing there and staring. What should I do?
Love from your son

DEAR SON

Well, what did you think of? Don't keep me in suspense on the slaughter bench! Tell me what you did. Because you must have thought up something cunning?
Love from anxious Mother

DEAR MOTHER

'Hush!' I said to them. 'Now you have exposed me! You are clever, you two. But don't tell anyone! Come here and taste! We can share!'

Then Where and Wherefore came up beside me and nosed in the hay. But suddenly they whirled round and ran out. What was I to do? Should I hide? Or should I run after them and get them to come back with me? They were my best friends, after all!

No, I just stood there, eating.
Love from your son

DEAR SON

But tell me, then, my little boy! What happened? They haven't killed you, have they?

DEAR MOTHER

I just had to cry a little before I went on with the story. I stood there eating as much as I could, and after a while the door flew open with a crash. It was Vera who stood there, my good friend, the largest of the ewes. At first she just stood blinking a little in the half-darkness. Then she snorted so fiercely through her nose that I dropped what I had in my mouth and ran into the corner to hide. But Vera ran towards me and shoved me right into the wall. I screamed and got up on my feet, but she shoved me down again.

'Mamma!' I yelled.

I was only a hungry little calf. But Vera didn't bother about that. She chased me out of the house. Outside stood Veren, waiting. He shoved me further away, away. Then he and the other sheep ran into the house. In a twinkling they had eaten it all up. Then they came out again and were just as hungry and just as bad-tempered. Vera and Veren ran after me and chased me far into the darkest forest. Here I stand now in the snow, nibbling at a birch tree.

Love from your son

DEAR SON

You must just be pleased that you survived when the sheep attacked you. They could have crushed both your guts and legs with their hard skulls. But now you surely understand that it won't work any longer. You have been lucky so far.

You found someone to be with, you had good friends, you even found a human to caress you for a while. And an old bundle of hay. But now it is finished! Yes, you have got more out of life in these weeks than many others manage in a whole life. You have experienced a lot that you can dream about. Enough for the rest of your life. Now you have only to come home again to the farm before the winter gets you! Listen to me for once!
Love from Mother

NO, MOTHER

I hear but I do not obey.

DEAR LOST SON!

Autumn is the worst of all seasons, but now the time of slaughter is over. I have told you that before. I said that all the bull calves had gone. But I was lying a bit, then, because there is a single bull calf left here. The one who was allowed to live is the son of Ringelihorn. He is called Brasse. But it could have been you who was spared. I am sure of that. You were much more hefty and broad across the chest than this troublemaker. At any rate now you can come safely down again to us. Then you can stay here at the farm and stand in the calf pen with Brasse. You will get plenty of space, and you can stand here at least until spring, anyway. Then you will be able to taste fresh green grass again. We have a

right to eight weeks' holiday in the home fields anyway every summer, even if life on the high pasture is finished. You can run away again early next autumn! My dear, you don't know what's good for you!
Your mother grieves

DEAR MOTHER

The whole world has become white! Yes, when I came out of the sheep shed early this morning the whole world was white. The snow lay thick over all the ground and all the bushes. Now I can't manage to dig down to the grass any more. But I was able to flounder through the snow over to a huge hazel bush. Under it I found some old leaves. And the bark of the hazel tastes better than birch. I ate and ate all day. My stomach is bursting, but I never feel properly full.
Love from your son, hungry and cold

MY DEAR LITTLE BOY

Come home! Don't torture yourself any longer. Come home while you are still able to walk!
Your mother forever

NO, MOTHER

I can surely stand being hungry for another couple of days. I lie quietly for long hours chewing the cud of lichen and moss. Oh, now it has come up again, the cushion of green moss I found earlier today, I say to myself. It fills my belly well! I'll have pleasure in that cushion of moss many times!

Last night rain came instead of snow. The snow has settled down a bit, and I can kick my way down to the tufts of grass. Perhaps the whole meadow will be green tomorrow?
Your son

DEAR SON

You poor thing, having to go around alone like that, suffering!

DEAR MOTHER

I am a bull who can cry, Mother. This is what it is like to be alone: I stand gazing straight at the wall, and the wall is grey and lifeless, and I feel grey and cold and lifeless through and through, and think grey thoughts about the good life I should have lived, sweet dreams about Mamma who is licking my neck, because I need it so badly, and when she says I have become too big for such things, then another one will come and lick me on the chest, a beautiful heifer of my own age, because I need it, and while I stand longing like this, it suddenly brightens up for me. At last something happens. At last somebody comes. Who is it?

Out of a crack in the grey wall of planks a little fly comes creeping, no, not little, she is big as flies go, she walks stiff-legged, and she hums so nicely with her wings, and the peaceful sound reminds me of the flies at home in the cowshed, and I blow warmth onto the fly to revive her, and I am very happy about this creature who will be company for me, she has six legs and I have four, but it doesn't matter, she has wings and I would like to have had them too, but it doesn't matter, because now the fly has no more energy, now the fly tumbles down, she lands on her back in the snow and lies there, spinning and spinning, she has a shock from the cold and is kicking with all her six legs, but it doesn't help, she has finished her whole fly life, soon lifeless, frozen to death, and I think that you let go quietly and easily, you tiny thing. But maybe you were forewarned, maybe you had felt it inside you for a long time?

I stood there and felt an impulse to stamp on the poor fly. I wanted to see her bleed. She had cheated me. But I didn't do it. I just stood there alone, facing the grey wall. It was I who was bleeding.

## BUT MY DEAR

Have you hurt yourself? Are you bleeding? Or are you raving? Are your feet twitching? Are you foaming at the mouth? Are you rubbing yourself until you bleed against that wall you mention?

Answer quickly!

HI MOTHER

You don't understand me. No, I haven't got the rubbing sickness. No, the sheep haven't infected me, and blood is not pouring out of me. I am just so lonely.
Love from me

DEAR SON

Thank goodness! How you scare an old hide! Would you like to hear something nice? One morning the farmer came in here to us with four buckets full of apples. They were crunchily delicious and juicy. We stood all lined up here in the warmth, chomping apples. This is what late autumn is like down here in the warmth! Then we got a big bowl of feed concentrates. And to finish off, a big bundle of hay each, which we could stick our noses deep into and enjoy. Oh you, how well off we are!
Love from Mother

NO, MOTHER

Don't try! I'm not so easily fooled. 'All lined up', yes. You can say that!
Free son

LITTLE SON

Don't you believe me? That wasn't all. Early this morning something quite unbelievable happened. Well, you can believe whatever you like. But there came the farmer, dragging a big black blob of something after him. He dragged this blob past all the other cows and right over to my place. Then he released me from the chain and asked me to step aside. I stood with big eyes, watching while he spread the black blob over the floor of my stall. Then he asked me to step up onto it. I refused. The blob stank. It smelled neither of animal nor human. It must be a cow trap, I thought. My time has come and he wants to get me into that sticky paste, I thought. So I flatly refused. But he coaxed and pulled me, he himself climbed up onto the black stuff and jumped up and down, he lay down and kicked his legs about. I hadn't expected that of the farmer, and then I gave in, I climbed up. Well, my goodness, my hooves sank in! It was as soft as a grassy plain on a wet autumn day.

A little later I lay down to rest. Then it first occurred to me, what it meant. The farmer wanted me to be soft and comfortable and lie down for a long time, resting in my old age. Not scraping my bones on the hard cement. Not wearing out my knees and hips. He came in several times and peeped at me and smiled in satisfaction when he saw I was lying on the mat in my stall.

The other cows couldn't make any sense of it. What had I done to ingratiate myself with the farmer? Had I given double milk or double cream? Oh no, rather less and thinner. He had chosen me all the same.

A happy cow

DEAR MOTHER

Good for you, Mother! You deserve to lie on a soft bed. Now I remember how apples taste. And how they crunch.
Your son

MY DEAR SON

Yes, I lay there thinking that the farmer had realized I was someone quite unique. But some days later I came down to earth again. Because then the farmer and a strange man came along, dragging stall mats for the whole herd. There was a terrible racket with shaking of chains and mooing and yelling and jostling and shifting here and there. But then all and everyone was in place. The cowshed stank worse than ever, but we were sure to get used to the stink. Soon there was only sighing and pleasant sounds to be heard. What a good-hearted man! Everyone praised the farmer. How could we thank him?
Your mother in the warmth

DEAR MOTHER

Do you know what happened today? No, you couldn't imagine it. Because suddenly Where and Wherefore turned up! I was dozing and was startled when I saw them. How big they had grown! Was it Where and Wherefore? Or was it Vera and Veren? I was ready to run away. But they just stood there shaking their tails, without a sound. Then they took me to a secret place under some large spruce trees. It was actually a little green warm hollow, down at the bottom of a steep gully, with a little spring that trickled out from between moss-grown rocks. There lay the other sheep, chewing the cud. No bleating or harsh words when I arrived. They just looked at me as I came tagging along behind the other two. I wagged my tail as well as I could, and was actually allowed to be in peace.

No, the water in the spring was not trickling, it was frozen to ice. But in between moss and roots, I found a fresh green cuckoo's meat which I gobbled up. Then the three of us lay down close together with me in the middle. I fell asleep like that.
Your son in the warmth

DEAR SON

Oh, it did me good, what you told me. At last I could relax! I saw you so clearly before me, lying soft and warm between the sheep.
Love from Mother

DEAR MOTHER

But when I woke up, Where and Wherefore had gone. The warm hollow and the cuckoo's meat and all the sheep. Nobody left, all over again.
Love from your son

NO NO NO

You must think of your mother, worrying here at home! Am I not to get peace soon?
Your mother

DEAR MOTHER

I do think about you, and I dream all sorts of strange things. I dream that flies are crawling in and out of my nostrils. But when I wake up, they have gone. I dream that the flies are standing close to each other in the corner of my eye, drinking the moisture. But when I wake up, I am alone. I dream about you, that you are coming stamping through the snow, big and warm and strong, to save me. But you are standing tied up in your stall. You are standing on your stall mat. Then you lie down and feel as comfortable as can be.

Mother, we are powerless, aren't we? We can't even hurt a fly. But humans can. They do as they like with us and all other living beings. They change us so we become exactly as they want us to be. Meat in the stall. Milk in the pail. That is all.
Cold son

MY DEAR CALF

Now you are not to burrow down in sad thoughts, or you will get nowhere. Be strong. Dream good dreams!
Your mother forever

## DEAR MOTHER

I have run away, but I am helpless out in freedom. I can dream away, but I wake up again and am just as helpless. I can go home again, so that I can stand in the warmth of the cowshed through the winter with you. Until we are both turned into meat.

What can we do about it? We who can't hurt a fly. Yes, while we are waiting in the stalls, we can try to whisk midges and flies away with our tails. We can do that. We can carry on all day long, but the same fly will come flying back a thousand times, a thousand times. It settles wherever it likes. We can twitch our skins and flap our ears and kick our feet. But nothing is of any use.

Your son, powerless

## YES, SON

I must say you are right. We are powerless. The farmer, on the other hand, knows how to handle everything. Once he came into the cowshed with a yellow strip which he hung from the ceiling. And the flies came swarming to it by the dozen. They let themselves be tricked. There they sat fast in the stickiness. They sat in thick black clusters, helplessly caught. I have seen this.

Cow proposes, man disposes.

Your mother

DEAR MOTHER

There are no flies in heaven, Mother.
Black calf

DEAR WISE SON

No, that is true. Up there everything is good. And when one day the Heavenly Cow comes down to us and turns the whole earth into green grazing grounds, all will be good here too.
Your mother

DEAR MOTHER

That was not what I meant. If the Heavenly Cow had experienced what it is like to have flies crawling upon her from morning to night, she would have done something about it. Maybe blessed us with a better tail which we could have slapped them dead with. Yes, Mother, if the Heavenly Cow had ever experienced what it is like to freeze and starve, she would have helped me now.
Black calf in white snow

DEAR SON

Come in spring. We must learn to be patient.
Mother

DEAR MOTHER

I woke up, freezing. I tried to sleep myself warm again, but couldn't. I only dreamed that I was getting even colder and I shivered all over. It felt as if I had been asleep for several days at a stretch, but I was not rested, only tired and limp. I ate a little heather which was sticking out of the snow. I wanted to shit, but only hard lumps came out. Then I started walking. I slipped. My hooves skidded. But the snow was deep and wet. I sank far down. Luckily, I have long legs. I could see the tracks of the sheep and tried to jump after them.

Where and Wherefore have gone this way, I thought. Those two are waiting for me a little further ahead. Look, there are sheep droppings, warm and fresh!

But the sheep droppings were only white snow, and I became more and more exhausted. I couldn't jump in the snow, I could hardly walk. Now and then I lay floundering in snow right up to my belly. The cold crept deep inside me, and I wanted only to lie in total peace, sleep and dream myself far away. Dream about hay and warmth, and about you, Mother. Come and lick my neck, Mamma! I need it.
Your son, the youngest one

DEAR MOTHER

After I had rested a bit and gathered strength, I began floundering onwards. It was snowing all the time. Where should I go? It was long since the snow had covered all the tracks of the wild sheep. I moaned, I called out to Where and Wherefore, but my voice sounded so strange and weak that I was frightened. Now and then I stopped and stretched out my neck, I was thirsty for teat-warm milk and opened

my mouth. But the white stuff that came dripping, landing on my tongue, was cold, tasteless as water, totally lacking in sweet taste and nutrition. This was how I had stood the first time I was given milk in a pail. My head stretched upwards, all by itself! My mouth searched upwards for your teats, but the farmer pressed my muzzle down into the pail. Then I smelled the scent of milk, and at once my head stretched upwards! I wanted to suck! No, I didn't understand anything at that time, and now I understand even less. What is happening? Aren't you going to save me soon?
Your son

DEAR MOTHER

The snow melted down my sides and made me frozen stiff all through. Thick clumps of snow hang, dangling in the shaggy hair under my belly. My dick shrivelled. He who had always dingle-dangled so freely and finely. No, what was there was useless. If Moonshine had popped up right in front of my nose, I wouldn't have had much to show for it.

I didn't see tracks any longer. But there was blood in my own tracks. I was bleeding between my hooves. It was stinging. I lay just breathing out and dreaming for long hours. I dreamed that the wolf came creeping up my bloody tracks. I had no energy to escape. But then I dreamed that I was smelling the scent of the cowshed.

Just one more jump, I said to myself, just three little steps more! Then I slept again.
Your son

DEAR MOTHER

After a long time I came out onto a big white plain. But what was that? Right in the middle of the plain stood a pail, with a handle and all! I jumped closer. Who had put a pail down there? I didn't see any footprints. Only snow everywhere. Carefully I went closer to the pail. It was snowing, and when I got there, I saw that a little snow lay in the bottom of the pail. Anyway I stuck my nose down into it. It smelled of milk! I stuck my nose right down and slurped. It tasted of milk, and the milk was good and warm!
Love from your son, with the taste of milk in his mouth

DEAR MOTHER

As soon as I had drunk that sip at the bottom of the pail, I felt warm and much fitter. But after a bit as I walked, I got colder and colder again. Now I am ice-cold, so cold that my body and feet ache. But the snow has become hard. I can walk on top of the hard white surface. I am walking up and up, over and over large white surfaces.

There isn't one green blade up here. Not a single bush which I could gnaw the bark of. No tracks of other animals. No, there can't be anyone but me in this white world.

What should I do? I bend down and lick the snow. The snow melts in my mouth, and on the way down my throat the melting water becomes milk. I believe it. But I am freezing. I am ice-cold even inside my stomach.
Your son

DEAR MOTHER

I tottered onwards. The clouds floated away. It stopped snowing. The sky cleared. The shining button on one of the Heavenly Cow's horns came into sight.

A little later I discovered a new pail, and I ran as fast as I could towards it. Guess if I was happy! The pail was full of steaming warm milk, and I yelled Mamma, Mamma! Then I slurped the milk. The warmth spread from my mouth down into my stomach. The lumps of ice in my stomach melted. The good warmth spread all over my body, my feet became strong and warm again, full of new energy. Who was I? I was a strong young calf wandering through the wide world! But was it you who had put the milk out for me? Or was it the Heavenly Cow?

I saw footprints in the snow around the pail. They were hoofprints, like my own. Other calves had been there and drunk, just before me! All the same the pail was full when I arrived.

Your son

DEAR MOTHER

I drank the pail empty and felt so strong and wild and happy that I began to run. I was no longer cold, and I wasn't at all afraid! I just ran onwards, so lightly. Far ahead I saw something moving. Yes, it was someone mooing! In the middle of the world of snow a huge herd of bull calves stood waiting. Brown, white, spotted or black like me.

It was all your bull calves, Mamma, and you can be proud! They were handsome, as handsome as the wild cattle of Africa! I was the smallest but I wasn't nervous. I just ran right into the herd.

'We have been waiting for you,' they said and licked my face.

Yes, they licked my face and my neck and along my sides, there were so many of them that they could lick all over my body, and I stood there and felt that I had arrived, I was home, I was warm and safe and good.

Your son, one of the many

DEAR MOTHER

Then we started walking. Oh, how I enjoyed it! I was strong and full of food and warmth, and I would never feel lonely again! Then I was so happy that I had to caper in a calf-dance! Calf-dance! With that all the other calves began jumping and dancing. You should have seen us! How fit and feisty we were!

While I was there dancing in the middle of the herd, I felt that someone was looking at us. Was someone up in the blue and white sky with us? I stole a glance upwards. Then I could see! I could see both the sun and the moon at the same time! Both the shining buttons on the Heavenly Cow's horns!

Calf-dance! Oh, how playfully, lightly we jumped and danced. Up over the plains and hills towards the Heavenly Cow we danced, all your sons together.

# A NOTE ON NAMES

More than 90% of the 355,000 Norwegian cows have names, indicating the close relationship between farmer and animal. The most common names are based on tradition, while new and inventive names are constantly being introduced. Names may be chosen due to colour, patches or behaviour, while some cows are named after celebrities, such as Diana, Kleopatra and Fabiola. In this story, 12 traditional cow names are used, while the names of the mother, the father and the calf have been coined by the author.

## ABOUT THE WHITE NIGHTS SERIES

On behalf of Vani Book Company and Vani Prakashan, we're happy to announce, retrospectively, the formal launch of the series White Nights with the publication of the English translations of the celebrated Norwegian poet and novelist Ingrid Storholmen's novel *Here Lay Tirpitz* and *Hans Sande's Black Calf @ White Snow*. Though we hadn't given the series this name earlier, White Nights, is nevertheless, already a substantial series rolled out by Vani Prakashan, of Scandinavian literature in Hindi translation. It goes without saying that we've been building up the series, straw by straw, first in Hindi, since the beginning of the millennium, with a major and voluminous publication of Swedish poetry and the works of the Nobel Prize-winning Norwegian novelist Knut Hamsun. The series also includes plays by Henrik Ibsen followed by several titles of contemporary Swedish poetry and Norwegian fiction. It is a labour of love for and our recognition of the significance of writing from these breathtakingly beautiful countries of northern Europe. So it's not that writers like Olav Hauge and Jon Fosse are with us because they are iconic names the world over, but because, in our view, their appearance in the Indian publishing scene is likely to have immense discursive value too, apart from introducing to Indian readers authors whose works bring incomparable, brand new and infinitely enriching reading experiences.

The series may well be regarded as a tribute to Fyodor Dostoevsky whose story 'White Nights' inspired its name. The young female protagonist of the story is shocked to hear that the man she happens to have befriended on a particularly magical white night is not in possession of the story of his life. When he asks her equally surprised, 'But who told you there was such a story?' she asks another baffling question: 'But how did you manage to live, if there's no story?' Between these two questions from 'White Nights', contemporary Nordic literature unveils its Janus-faced existence: the wholesome classical story-telling and the infinitely evocative fragmentary writing, both of which seem to possess an equally compelling incantatory quality in most texts we've been taking up for publishing. What might distinguish Nordic writing further is the utterly mysterious blending of these faces, at times, in the body of the same text, when in the mystery of an un-dark night or a dark winter day illumined only by snow-light, the faces slowly turn around to face each other!

I am happy to find a publication team that chose to be counted among the pioneers in Indian publishing in their willingness to venture into the Hindi as well as English translations of significant works from Norwegian and Swedish literature. The Hindi already occupies decent shelf space and enjoys considerable readership in our country warranting many a title to go into subsequent editions. Now the English translations are also lined up for publication, and, in some cases, we have the same authors or/and titles that will appear in both languages. The Nordic series in

English translation is in the making and that's what seems to matter most of all to us at this given moment in the history of Indian publishing.

**Teji Grover**
Series Editor

## ALSO IN WHITE NIGHTS

HERE LAY TIRPITZ
a novel

Ingrid Storholmen
Translated from the Norwegian
by Marietta Taralrud Maddrell

'This is a disturbing and strong anti-war novel. It is seldom that such great sorrow and pain is told so sparingly and intensely. Highly recommended!'—*Adresseavisen*

In this stunning novel, acclaimed Norwegian poet Ingrid Storholmen resurrects the lives, trials and dreams of the men on board Tirpitz, the largest battleship of Hitler's navy, and that of their wives, lovers, family and the local Norwegians who encountered the ship—with profound immediacy and grace. Through monologues, conversations and letters Stormholen traces the personal journeys of those caught in the war. Young farmhands like Otto—hopeful about escaping anonymity and starting a new life; educated skeptics like Kaspar—forced to enlist to keep his father out of jail; fascists like Carl—fighting for the purity of the Aryan race; young Norwegian women like Berit—who swaps thankless domestic drudgery for shipyard cleaning; among countless others.

*Here Lay Tirpitz* is an immersive chorus of voices waiting for life to begin, or death. It shows us the beauty, vulnerability—and ugliness—of men and women, in a world overrun by hatred and power. Now, when such forces are in ascendance yet again, Storholmen reminds us of the human cost of war. In this scintillating English translation, we have a timely masterpiece: audacious, sensuous and devastating.